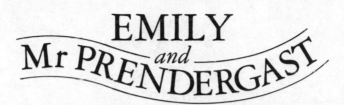

ORCHARD
ReadAlouds

EMILY and Mr PRENDERGAST

Shirley Isherwood

ILLUSTRATED BY
Dorothy Tucker

ORCHARD
BOOKS
LONDON & NEW YORK

For my dear husband,
Geoffrey Isherwood

But if the while I think on thee, dear friend,
All losses are restored and sorrows end.

WILLIAM SHAKESPEARE

Text copyright © Shirley Isherwood 1989
Illustrations copyright © Dorothy Tucker 1989
First published in Great Britain in 1989 by
ORCHARD BOOKS
10 Golden Square, London W1R 3AF
Orchard Books, Australia
14 Mars Road, Lane Cove, New South Wales 2066
1 85213 033 4
Printed in Great Britain

Contents

1

Mr Prendergast

Once upon a time there was a little girl called Emily, who had a cat who could speak. He was known as Thomas — but his real name was Mr Prendergast.

He was a very beautiful cat. His coat was striped, his feet were white, and his eyes were a deep golden yellow. He was given to Emily on her birthday, and it was on the evening of the birthday party that he first spoke to her.

"You're a very nice present!" said Emily, when all the guests had gone home, and she was alone with her cat.

"Yes, I am," said Mr Prendergast.

"Who gave you to me?" asked Emily. She had received a great many presents, but she couldn't remember anyone giving her a cat.

"*I* gave me to you!" said Mr Prendergast. He sounded rather offended.

"Oh, yes! Now I remember," said Emily, quickly — for she did not wish to offend Mr Prendergast. "It was very kind of you."

"Please don't mention it," said Mr Prendergast. "But you really ought to say, 'Thank you for your unusual and useful gift'. Or you may prefer to write a thank you note."

So Emily wrote a thank you note and gave it to him, and after that they became good friends.

It was wonderful to have Mr Prendergast as a friend, and Emily loved him dearly. He told her many interesting stories, and he danced for her in the long grass at the bottom of the garden. (Sometimes he sang, but his singing wasn't as good as his dancing.) But, because he wouldn't speak to anyone but Emily, he got her into a great deal of trouble. It was hard to explain why she did the things she did — for very often the idea had been Mr Prendergast's.

"I wish that you would speak to everyone and explain," said Emily. But Mr Prendergast said that it wouldn't do for him to speak to everyone. He said that he often lay awake at night, thinking about this problem; but Emily didn't believe him.

One day, when Mr Prendergast had been living with Emily for three weeks, Emily found that she had a new baby brother. Everyone said, "Oh, Emily! Aren't you pleased!" But Emily wasn't sure whether she was pleased or not.

Mr Prendergast wasn't pleased. He said "Phhttt!" and stalked off to the bottom of the garden, and didn't come back for two days.

On the day of the christening party, Emily was dressed in her best frock, and told to sit quietly in the dining room. "Don't touch anything," said her mother. "And whatever you do, don't get dirty."

Emily sat down on a chair, and Mr Prendergast sat down beside her. "The baby gets his name today," said Emily, "he will be called Daniel."

"*I think he should be called fish*," said Mr Prendergast, "because he reminds me of a fish I once ate . . . I mean, met."

"You can't call a person *fish*," said Emily. But Mr Prendergast wasn't listening. His eyes had grown narrow and he was purring quietly to himself. "I met him last Wednesday, on Westcombe Sands," he said. "He told me the story of his life."

"*Can* fishes tell you the story of their life?" asked Emily.

"Of course," said Mr Prendergast. "Every life has a story, and every story can be told."

He rose, and stretched himself, and arched his back. "We will take a little walk," he said. "We will not go far. Perhaps just to the next door garden. We will be back in time for the christening tea."

Emily jumped down from her chair.

"Before we set off," said Mr Prendergast, "take one of the napkins from the table. I fear I may have caught a cold, and it is prudent to cover the shoulders when one has a cold."

Emily took a napkin from the table, and tied it round Mr Prendergast's shoulders. "Also, take some of the silver balls from the trifle," said Mr Prendergast, "and I will teach you a game which is played with silver balls and buttercups."

So Emily took some silver balls from the trifle, which had been set out for the christening tea. Then

together she and Mr Prendergast went over the garden. The lawn hadn't been mown for a long time; it was full of buttercups and daisies, and the long grass tickled Emily's legs as she went. "Take off your shoes," said Mr Prendergast, "and let your feet be tickled too. It is good for the toes and it also helps to keep your shoes clean."

So Emily took off her shoes. The day was warm and dry, and the dust of the path covered her feet and Mr Prendergast's shawl. "I will tell you the tale of my friend, the fish," said Mr Prendergast, as they strolled along. "He was stranded in a large pool on

15

the beach. However, he liked it so much that he decided that he would not go back to sea. He now lives at number forty-two."

"Next door?" said Emily, in surprise.

"Yes," said Mr Prendergast, "and see — the door is open. We will pay him a visit!"

Before Emily could stop him, he ran through the gap in the hedge, and into the house. Emily ran after him, dropping her shoes. "Mr Prendergast! Mr Prendergast!" she called as she went.

She found him, some moments later, in the living room of number forty-two. He was standing on his hind legs, before the large tank of fish, and dabbling about in the water with his paw. "There he is!" he said, as he swished the water about.

"Oh, Mr Prendergast," said Emily, "let's go home!" But Mr Prendergast just reached deeper into the tank, and his white curved claws appeared at the end of his paw.

Emily stood and held her breath. Then she grabbed Mr Prendergast firmly round his middle, and ran with him, back to her own garden.

"Phhttt!" said Mr Prendergast angrily, when she

put him down; then, shaking his wet leg, he ran off and disappeared into the long grass. Emily followed the tip of his tail, but soon she lost sight of him altogether. After a time, she came across the white napkin, lying in a clump of clover. It was creased and dirty and there was a small tear in one corner.

"Oh, phhttt!" said Emily. She folded the napkin up, and went a little further, and at last found her cat. He was sitting by the garden shed and he looked angry and offended.

Emily held out the napkin, but Mr Prendergast turned his head away. "It's dirty," he said. "I refuse to wear a dirty shawl."

Emily sat down beside him, and took the silver balls from her pocket, but Mr Prendergast was no longer interested. "What's the matter?" asked Emily.

"Nothing at all," said Mr Prendergast. Then he rose and began to stroll away. "I rather think that your shoes have arrived," he said, as he vanished into the long grass once more. Emily looked up and saw her mother coming down the path with Emily's shoes in her hand. She didn't look very pleased.

Emily gazed down at her dusty feet and her grass-stained frock and sighed. Once again Mr Prendergast had got her into trouble; and again it was almost impossible to say exactly what had happened. One thing had simply led to another.

That night, as Emily lay in bed, she saw the black shape of her cat sitting on the window sill. "Mr Prendergast," she whispered, and he came through the open window and sat down on her pillow. "Tell me the fish's tale," she said.

"I'm afraid that I've forgotten it," said Mr Prendergast. "This is what one finds. Fish and their tales are soon forgotten."

18

"Their *tales* or their *tails?*" said Emily.

"Both," said Mr Prendergast. Then he leapt from her bed, and disappeared into the night. Emily lay back on her pillow, and when she turned her head, she saw that he had placed three silver balls and a crumpled buttercup on the bedcover. "But what do I *do* with them?" she said to herself. "He forgot to tell me how to play the game!" Then, before she could think any more on the matter, she fell fast asleep.

2

Travelling

It was time for Mr Prendergast to visit the vet. He was going to have an injection, so that he wouldn't get cat 'flu. Emily carried the travelling basket out into the garden, and showed it to him; but he merely sniffed at it suspiciously, then scrambled up to the top of the tree. So Emily went into the kitchen and made him a special treat of sardines, set out on his plate in the shape of a star. Then she set the plate in the grass, beneath the tree. The silver sardines shone in the sun and, just as she expected, Mr Prendergast came down from his branch. "Oh, starry fishes!" he said happily.

Emily sat and watched him, and sighed. It is never pleasant to deceive a friend, even if you do it with the best of intentions. "I'm doing it for your own *good*," she said, and she pounced on him, while the last of the little fishes still dangled from his mouth, and popped him into the basket. Then she closed the lid quickly, and fastened the two leather straps.

Inside the basket, Mr Prendergast began to turn round and round. The paper which lined the bottom of the basket made a rustling sound, Mr Prendergast himself hissed, and altogether it was more like having a trapped snake than a cat. Emily became alarmed, and knelt down before the basket. "Mr Prendergast," she said, "you are just going travelling."

As soon as she said this, Mr Prendergast became calmer. Peering at him through the little gaps in the wicker work, Emily saw a pleased smile spread over his face. "Travelling?" he said. "Then I must have a label for my basket with 'Mr Prendergast — Travelling' written on it," he said.

So Emily went into the house and asked her mother to make a label. When it was tied to the lid of the basket, everyone began to make their way up the hill to the village station. Daniel travelled in a sling, which Emily's mother wore round her shoulder. He slept for most of the walk — and, to Emily's surprise, Mr Prendergast slept too, and slid in a great furry heap from one end of his basket to the other. He was very heavy, and Emily was glad when they reached the station, and she could put the basket down on a bench.

At once, Mr Prendergast awoke, and began to push up the corner of the basket lid with his head. "Have we *arrived?*" he said. "Have we reached our *destination?*" He began to scrabble wildly with his paws, and a wedge of his tabby face appeared, with his ears flattened back. "Journey's end!" he said.

"No, it isn't!" said Emily. "The journey has hardly begun yet! She put her hand on the basket lid, and gently pushed it back into place.

Mr Prendergast lay down, and Emily saw the gleam of his golden eye through the basket-work. He was gazing at the station flowerbeds, where the station master grew pink and white carnations. "A gentleman, when travelling," he said, "ought to have a flower in his buttonhole."

"But you aren't a gentleman," said Emily, "and you don't have a buttonhole."

At this, Mr Prendergast began to push up the corner of the lid once more. He was surprisingly strong, and seemed determined to get out. "I am a gentleman *cat*," he said.

Emily glanced to where her mother sat at the other end of the bench, talking to a friend, then she ran to the flowerbed, picked a carnation, and pushed it under the basket lid.

"Thank you," said Mr Prendergast. "Now may I have my ticket, please."

"Your ticket!" said Emily.

"Of course," said Mr Prendergast. "Everyone who travels should have a ticket. It tells you the name of your destination — in case you take a little nap and forget where you are going. 'Ah-ha!' you cry, taking out your ticket, *'that's* where I'm going — India!'"

At this, Mr Prendergast pushed up the lid of the basket once more, and he and Emily looked at one another.

"Where *are* we going, by the by?" Mr Prendergast asked.

"I've forgotten," she said.

Emily didn't like to tell him that he was only on his way to the vet's, so she went to her mother, and asked to be allowed to hold the tickets. Then she gave one to Mr Prendergast, who took it between his little white teeth, and disappeared with it into the basket.

Emily breathed a sigh of relief; but a moment later the corner of the lid rose again. "Timetable!" said Mr Prendergast. "All travellers must have a timetable. It helps with the connections."

"Connections!" said Emily.

"How one train connects with another," explained

24

Mr Prendergast, with great patience. " 'Ha-ha!' you cry, looking at your timetable, 'the eleven o'clock arrives on platform one, and the eleven-five goes from platform three — I've just got time to *make the connection*.' Then, grabbing your bag, you leave the eleven o'clock train, and run as fast as you can to platform three."

The corner of the lid rose higher and higher as he spoke, and he looked exactly like a worried traveller, anxious that his journey should go smoothly.

"I'll get you a timetable!" said Emily, afraid that he would escape from his basket. She ran into the little station hall, where the timetables were arranged in rows on a little wooden rack, took one of each kind, and hurried back to Mr Prendergast.

The timetables seemed to excite him a great deal — for when Emily slid them beneath the basket lid, he gathered them together and began to knead them with his two front paws. "The twelve-fifteen from Stokehampton!" he said. "Buffet and dining cars available — except on Sundays."

"Mr Prendergast!" said Emily, trying to calm him; but there was no time to say more, for the train had come into the station. Emily followed her mother into a carriage, and set the basket down on a seat. Outside, on the platform, the station master blew his whistle, and the train began to move. In his basket, Mr Prendergast shouted loudly, "Change at Mortlake!", and then, abruptly, fell asleep.

Mr Prendergast slept all through the train journey. He slept as Emily carried him along the platform — but when they reached the ticket barrier, Emily had to confess that one of the tickets lay in Mr Prendergast's basket.

"Oh, Emily!" said Emily's mother.

The basket was opened, and Mr Prendergast awoke.

The hall of the station was covered with a great dome of coloured glass, and as Mr Prendergast awoke and sat up in his basket, the sun shone through the glass, and made shafts of light. At the same time a street musician began to play his flute, and the two things together, the light and the music, caused a kind of magic spell to fall over the station and the travellers. Then Mr Prendergast himself became part of the magic, as he jumped

from his basket, and trotted through the hall.
"What a beautiful cat!" said the travellers, as he
made his way through the blue and golden lights. A
porter started after him, but Emily caught his arm.
"Please let him stay," she said, "just for a little. He
thinks he's in India."

Mr Prendergast went round the station hall. He
stopped to sniff at the bunches of flowers that stood
in buckets outside the florist stall. He wound himself
round the ankles of the man who sold newspapers.

He sat and read the luggage labels on suitcases. Travellers bent and stroked his head, and it was as if they had come to the station not to catch trains or to be met by friends and relatives, but just to see Mr Prendergast. Then the shafts of light faded, the music ended, and the magic fled. Emily picked up Mr Prendergast, and put him back in the basket. "India is a delightful place!" he said, as she closed the lid.

Emily said nothing to this; how can you tell a friend that he is not in a faraway land, but merely on his way to visit the vet?

At the vet's, Mr Prendergast was carried away by a nurse in a white coat. In a very short time he came back, crouched down in his basket, with all four paws tucked under him. Emily lifted a corner of the basket lid and looked at him. "I shall pretend that this never happened," he said, in his iciest tones; then he closed his eyes and went to sleep.

Mr Prendergast slept all through the journey home. When they reached the house, Emily carried the basket out into the garden. She felt a little nervous. All the way home she had been planning what she was going to say to Mr Prendergast. She thought of many things, but in the end decided to say simply this: "I'm sorry I tricked you — *but it was for your own good.*"

But as the basket lid fell back, she was surprised to see that he wasn't at all angry. He wasn't even slightly annoyed. His eyes were large and dark, and he stepped gently from the basket and slowly made his way over the garden. "India . . . India . . ." he said dreamily as he went.

Emily followed him, and watched as he climbed a tree, and sat on a low branch. "I am a great traveller," he said, gazing down at her, "I have been round the world."

"No, you haven't," said Emily, but Mr Prender-gast didn't hear her. "I may write a book about my travels," he said, closing his eyes, and purring loudly. "It will be very exciting. It will go like this: Chapter One. I set out on my journey . . ."

He really did seem to have forgotten all about his visit to the vet. He also seemed to have forgotten the fact that he had slept in his basket through most of the journey. But that didn't matter, thought Emily, as she made her way back down the garden. He had enjoyed his travels; he had seen a beautiful place, and it didn't matter at all what name he gave to it. She bent and picked up the basket, with the label, the crumpled carnation and the tattered timetables. "Chapter Two. I arrive in India . . ." she heard him say, as she went into the house for tea.

3

Mr Prendergast's Holiday

Emily was going on holiday with her mother and father. They were going to spend a week at the seaside. Mr Prendergast went to stay at a holiday home for cats. It was a pleasant place, and there Mr Prendergast was given a little green house, all to himself, with a plot of grass in which grew marigolds and daisies. On either side of his little house stood other small green houses, and each little plot and house was covered by a high cage of wire netting.

Emily said goodbye to Mr Prendergast a little tearfully, for she felt that she was putting him into a prison. But he just strolled off, quite unconcerned, and went to sit on the roof of his holiday house.

Emily had a wonderful time at the seaside. The sun shone every day, and she paddled in the sea, and made sandcastles. But often as she stood with the little waves about her feet, she thought about Mr Prendergast, and wondered what he was doing.

At the end of the week Emily and her father went to bring Mr Prendergast home. He didn't seem to be particularly pleased, but just came from his basket, and trotted off to the bottom of the garden. Emily ran after him, and found him sitting by the fence. He was busy washing himself, and he had the air of someone who has returned from a great adventure, and who is taking a bath, and thinking of all the things that they have done.

"Mr Prendergast," said Emily, "what have you been doing?"

"Doing?" said Mr Prendergast. "Don't you know? I sent you a postcard to tell you."

"I didn't get a postcard," said Emily.

"Then you must have one now," said Mr Prendergast.

Emily went back into the house, and found a postcard and a pencil. But when she went back into the garden, and laid these things before Mr Prendergast, he merely looked at her, and said, "*I* shall tell the story and *you* shall write it down."

Before Emily could say that she had only learned to write short words, he jumped up and began to pace back and forth.

"Monday," he said, "and the beginning of our adventures. Scraggs-Mulligan and I decided that we would take a sea voyage. But scarce were we out of sight of land than we saw the pirate ship! The crew paced the deck, hissing and spitting. 'Ha-ha!' cried Scraggs. 'Ho-ho!' cried I, and seizing our swords we whirled them above our heads. The blades flashed in the sun . . . ."

"Mr Prendergast!" cried Emily, but he just stared at her with narrow eyes. "Write it all down," he said.

Emily did her best. She wrote "Ha-ha" and she wrote "Ho-ho" — but she couldn't write seizing and whirling and spitting and hissing.

Mr Prendergast leant against her as she wrote. "The next day," he said, "Scraggs-Mulligan and I decided that we would climb a mountain. Up we went, past boulders and stones, through cracks and gulleys, over peaks and crags! Down came the wind! Flattened our ears! Bowled Scraggs over! 'Up!' I cried. 'On!' cried Scraggs . . . "

Then, carried away by the excitement of his tale, he jumped up and raced off over the garden. His words floated out behind him as he went. "Oh, the snow and the ice and the mysterious mist!" he said as he disappeared in the long grass.

It was a long time before Emily found him, but at last she came upon him, lying calmly by a clump of petunias. "Have you written it all down?" he said. Emily knelt beside him with the postcard on her knees. Holding the pencil tightly, she wrote "up" and "on". Mr Prendergast watched her as she wrote.

"The end of the story," he said. "We reached the top of the mountain, where we planted a small but tasteful flag."

The postcard was now rather dirty, and it was almost full, with just one small clean place left. "Shall I put 'love and kisses' on the bottom?" said Emily. She felt very pleased with herself, for she had done her best to write the story down.

Mr Prendergast jumped to his feet, and gazed at her in amazement. "Certainly not!" he said. "There is a great deal more to be said. We must describe to whom the adventure happened. It is the most important part of the story."

He began to pace about in front of her again. "You may describe me in your own words," he said. "But might I suggest the words 'striped', 'handsome', and 'graceful'."

But it was impossible for Emily to write these words, and so she just made little scribbly marks, shielding the postcard with her hand, so that Mr Prendergast couldn't see what she was doing.

"As for Scraggs," Mr Prendergast went on, smiling as he thought of his friend, "write that he is a large cat, massive of shoulder, bold of nature, and fierce in battle." The words tumbled from his lips so quickly that even if Emily had been able to write them there would scarcely have been time.

"Courageous," he said, going swish-swish-swish-through the long grass, "magnificent, jewel-eyed, broad-pawed." Then he stopped pacing, and flopped suddenly across her knee, bending the postcard as he did so. "I trust," he said, smiling up at her, "that you have described me in similar terms."

"I haven't described you at all," said Emily; for she felt now that it was best he know the truth. "I can't write long words. I've only written 'Ha-ha!' and 'Ho-ho!' and 'Flag'." She smoothed out the crumpled postcard and showed it to him. Mr Prendergast looked at it closely. "Do you mean," he said at last, "that you haven't written anything about the mysterious mist, or the swords in the sun? Do you mean that you haven't even added a few words of your own about our bravery?"

"But what should I have written?" asked poor Emily.

"You could have written 'Picture to yourself, dear

reader, these two bold animals!' "

"But Mr Prendergast," said Emily, "it isn't a *book*. It's only a postcard."

"But it could have been one of the best postcards in the whole world," said Mr Prendergast. He was very angry, and he said "Phhttt!" several times, and then stalked off over the garden. "I shan't tell you any more about my adventures", he said as he went.

"Well, I don't want to hear them," said Emily. "I don't believe them anyway!" For surely, she told herself, he couldn't have done any of the things he said he had done. He had been completely enclosed in wire netting for a whole week, and all he could have done was stroll about his little grassy plot, and sniff his marigolds.

For the rest of the day Emily wandered about the garden. She carried the postcard in her pocket, and from time to time she took it out and looked at it. It made her feel a little unhappy, for it does make you sad, to have tried your best to please, but find that you have failed to do so.

That night, when she went to bed, she took the

postcard with her and propped it by the side of her lamp, together with the pencil. Then she lay back on her pillow, and gazed at it. It would have been wonderful to be able to write Mr Prendergast's story, she thought, even if it wasn't true; it would be wonderful to be able to write words like "whirled" and "mysterious" and "magnificent" and "jewel-eyed".

As she lay, Mr Prendergast came through the open window and jumped on to her bed. "On Wednesday," he said, in his friendly voice, as though nothing had happened between them, "Scraggs and I went up in a balloon. Write it down."

Emily sat up. "But Mr Prendergast," she said, "I can't write balloon."

"Yes, you can," said Mr Prendergast, and he took the postcard gently between his teeth, and dropped it in her lap. "First you write 'ball'," he murmured in her ear, "and then you simply write 'oon'."

Holding the pencil tightly, Emily wrote "ball" and then "oon" — and there it was, the word "balloon". It was the longest word that she had ever written. "I've done it!" she said.

But Mr Prendergast just gazed past her, with wide, dark eyes. "Up and up we went," he said, "over fields and streams, cities and towns, until we reached the end of the land. And there you were, standing on the seashore."

"Oh, Mr Prendergast!" said Emily; for when he said this she knew that he must have been telling the truth after all. She *had* stood at the edge of the sea, with the little waves round her feet. "If I'd looked up," she said, "I would have seen you."

"But you didn't look up," said Mr Prendergast, "you just stood and thought about me."

He leapt from the bed and stood for a moment

on the window sill. "The postcard is finished," he said. "You may put all the kisses on the bottom now, if you wish."

And with that he was gone, down over the sloping roof of the kitchen, and along the garden fence. Emily wondered if he had gone to meet Scraggs-Mulligan; then she carefully made a row of kisses along the bottom of the postcard, put the postcard under her pillow, and fell fast asleep.

4

The Night Garden

It was a summer's night, and very hot indeed. Emily had awakened to see Mr Prendergast sitting on her window sill, between the white lace curtains. But even though the window was open, the curtains didn't move, for there was no breeze at all. Mr Prendergast looked as though he were sitting on a stage, and that the dark sky, the tree tops and the moon behind him was the scenery.

Emily sat up in bed and looked at him. "Please sing for me," she said.

"Very well," said Mr Prendergast, and he began to sing very softly.

"It's a hot summer's night, and I sing on the sill,
    I sing on the sill on this hot summer night,
And the hundreds and thousands of stars in the sky

Shine so bright that I wish, and I *wish* that I might . . .''

He stopped singing and stared at Emily.

"Might what?" asked Emily.

"Fly," said Mr Prendergast.

"Why do you wish to fly?" asked Emily.

"Because it rhymes with 'sky'," said Mr Prendergast.

"You can't wish for a thing because it rhymes," said Emily.

"It is as good a reason as any," said Mr Prendergast, coldly.

"Don't be cross," said Emily, and she got out of bed, and leant on the sill. Together, she and Mr Prendergast looked down on the garden.

"It looks different," said Emily. "In the dark, the garden is all changed."

"It is my night-garden," said Mr Prendergast. "The day-garden is your garden, but the night-garden is mine . . . and the lane, the field and the little wood," he added.

"Oh, Mr Prendergast," said Emily. "You are

lucky to have a night-garden."

"I am," said Mr Prendergast. "But I deserve it."
He wiped his left ear with his paw, and smoothed his
whiskers; which was what he always did before
setting off on one of his mysterious night errands.

"Please don't go!" said Emily.

Mr Prendergast looked at her. "I will sing you one
last song before I leave," he said, in his kindliest
voice; and sitting bolt upright, and swaying a little
from side to side, he began.

"Down in the night-garden, Emily dances,

Up through the long grass, down through the dark
grass,
And who shall know what Prendergast sees, as
Emily dances,
Up to her knees in the long grass, the dark grass,
While under the moon, Prendergast plays on the
flute
A sweet tune — and round and round, Emily goes,
Clocks in her hair, seeds in her toes . . ."

"*Clocks*!" said Emily as she and Mr Prendergast went quietly to the bedroom door and turned the knob. "In my *hair*?"

"*Dandelion* clocks," said Mr Prendergast.

"Do you really have a flute?" asked Emily, as she followed her cat through the door and out along the garden path. Mr Prendergast didn't answer.

The garden path looked very different at night: the bushes which grew on either side seemed thicker, and the moonlight made every bump and stone look bigger and quite beautiful. Even Mr Prendergast was changed. His coat was a different colour, and his eyes were darker.

"Oh, Mr Prendergast," said Emily, looking down at her bare moonlit feet. "We are different."

"Yes . . ." said Mr Prendergast. "That is correct . . ."

But he wasn't really listening to her — for suddenly he left her side and ran down the path a little way. Then he stopped and pounced. There was a high squealing sound from the long grass by the side of the fence. Mr Prendergast reappeared, licking his lips. "Field mouse," he said.

"Oh!" cried Emily angrily. "You've killed a mouse. Mr Prendergast, you're cruel."

But Mr Prendergast just sat by her side, purring. "I am Mr Prendergast *in the night*," he explained.

"Then I don't like you at night," said Emily. "I don't like you changed."

"Change is a good thing," said Mr Prendergast, calmly.

"No, it isn't," said Emily. "It was nice when you sang about dancing and about your flute — but now it's all spoiled."

"Phhttt," said Mr Prendergast. He leapt up on

the fence, and sat down. Beyond the fence was the lane and the field. "Please sing for me again," said Emily, looking out into the darkness, and feeling a little afraid.

"Very well," said Mr Prendergast, and he sang;

"Change is a flute playing
Now high, now low,
Now sad, now slow,
Change is Prendergast singing,
I am here now,
But soon I go . . ."

He jumped down from the fence and went off through the long grass. Emily followed him, seeing his moonlit tail swaying from side to side, and hearing him singing as he went.

"Change is the world turning,
Day to night;
Some things we do are wrong,
Some are right . . ."

And then he disappeared completely. "Don't leave

46

me!" cried Emily. The tree in the garden had turned into a tall witch, the moon was hidden behind a cloud, and the whole world was changed. "Mr Prendergast!" Emily shouted.

"Yes?" came the voice of Mr Prendergast, close by her right foot.

"Oh, Mr Prendergast," said Emily, "I thought you'd gone."

"Gone?" said Mr Prendergast. "It isn't time to go. It is time to dance. First I sing, then I hunt, and then I dance."

He ran a little way from her, and leapt up into the air, twisting his body as he rose. Then he arched his

back, jumped on all four feet, and danced across the garden.

After watching him for a little while, Emily began to dance with him. Round and round she whirled, until the garden, sky, stars and moon all spun and tilted. As she turned, she thought she heard the sound of music, and for a fleeting moment she saw Mr Prendergast sitting on a little knoll of grass, with the silver flute to his lips. But when she turned again, the flute was gone, and Mr Prendergast was sitting still and looking at her. "The dance has ended," he said.

Emily sat down beside him, and decided that she liked the world at night after all. But when the first drops of rain began to fall, Mr Prendergast said "Phhttt" very crossly.

"But it's lovely," said Emily. She held out her hand to catch the drops. The rain began to fall more quickly, then quicker still, and she got to her feet and began to skip in the cool, wet grass. "Sing a song about dancing in the rain," she said. But Mr Prendergast made no answer, and as the lightning flashed across the sky she saw him trotting up the path, with his tail held erect. Emily ran after him.

When she reached the kitchen, she found him sitting by the stove, washing a back leg. He was purring loudly, and his eyes were narrow as though he had just that moment woken up and the singing, the hunting and the dancing had never been.

"Oh, Emily," said Emily's mother, as Emily stood shivering in her wet pyjamas, "what *will* you do next?"

The next day Emily had a cold and stayed in bed. At noon Mr Prendergast came to visit her. He gazed at her calmly as she coughed and sneezed. Emily was annoyed. "You said that change was good," she said.

"Change for the *better*," said Mr Prendergast. "I thought *that* much was understood."

"Please sing for me," said Emily, who was tired of being in bed with nothing to do.

"I can't sing during the day," said Mr Prendergast. "Mine is a night voice only." And with that, he leapt from her bed, on to the window sill, down the sloping roof of the kitchen, and out into the sunny, daytime garden.

5

A Special Place

Mr Prendergast was very restless. He wandered about the house, going from room to room so quickly that Emily could hardly keep up with him. "Mr Prendergast," she said, when at last they met in the hall, "are you looking for mice?"

"Mice?" said Mr Prendergast. "*Mice?*" He seemed rather offended, and ran out of the house and along the path. Emily followed him to where he sat in the patch of long grass at the bottom of the garden. "Have you lost something?" she said, sitting down by his side.

Mr Prendergast stared at her with narrow yellow eyes. "One cannot lose something one has never had," he said.

"What have you never had?" asked Emily.

"A special place," said Mr Prendergast. "All cats have a special place, but I can't seem to find my own.

It is a very sad thing, to know that you have a special place, but not be able to find it."

As he spoke he let his striped body go limp, so that he lay over her knees, like a little fur rug. His purr grew louder, and he gazed steadily into her eyes. He wasn't to be trusted when he lay singing in her lap — Emily knew that; but it was lovely to think that somewhere there was a special place. "I'll help you find it!" she said.

Round the garden they went — but none of the places they found were special. At last they came back to the patch of long grass. "This is the place," said Mr Prendergast.

"We have been here before," said Emily, "and it wasn't special then."

"You can make it special," said Mr Prendergast.

"How?" asked Emily — but Mr Prendergast didn't answer her question. "In old Egyptian days," he said, "cats were thought to be gods. If I had lived in old Egyptian days I would have had a little temple. People would come to see me. 'Oh, great cat-god,' they would say, 'grant my dearest wish . . .'"

52

He swayed from side to side as he spoke, and then suddenly sat quite still and turned his head to look at her. "Which is why," he said, "all cats like to have a special place, where they can remember the time when they were gods."

"Oh, Mr Prendergast!" said Emily, "I'll make you a temple!" She ran into the house, took the big brass candlestick from the hall table, and carried it back to the bottom of the garden. It looked beautiful, standing in the grass and shining in the sun. But Mr Prendergast just glanced at it. "It is *almost* a temple," he said, "but I need one more beautiful thing."

Emily went back to the house, took the big blue china bowl from the table, and carried it carefully to Mr Prendergast. "Now your temple is finished," she said. She was very pleased, for it looked wonderful. The gold-shining candlestick, the blue bowl, and Mr Prendergast were all set about with long green blades of grass, and the grass was hung with spiders' webs and dandelion clocks. She had made an ordinary place into a place that was filled with magic, and she was caught in its spell.

But Mr Prendergast just sighed, and said, "The bowl should be filled with *water*."

So Emily went up and down the path, filling her little watering can at the kitchen sink, and carrying it down to the bottom of the garden. When the bowl was full she saw at once that Mr Prendergast was right. The water reflected their two faces, and while it is wonderful to feel that you are in a special place, and are somehow different, it is even better to be able to see yourself there. "Oh, Mr Prendergast," said Emily, happily, "we are two old Egyptians, sitting in your beautiful temple."

At this, Mr Prendergast raised his head, and looked at her. "*I* look like an Egyptian," he said, "but you do not."

"What does an Egyptian look like?" asked Emily — but Mr Prendergast would not say. His eyes were closed, and he seemed to have grown taller and thinner. The special place had changed him into a cat-god; but when Emily looked at her own face again in the water, she saw that she was still Emily, with her fair, fluffy hair lying against her forehead. "I haven't changed!" she said.

"You haven't tried," said Mr Prendergast. "One cannot change without trying."

Emily got up and ran into the house, to where her father sat reading a book in the big armchair. "Show me a picture of an old Egyptian!" said Emily.

Emily's father took a book from the bookcase, and showed her a picture of an Egyptian girl. She was small and slender, and she wore a dress with a pattern of stripes. Her fingers were hung with little bells and cymbals, and by her side was a cat who sat just as Mr Prendergast sat in his special place.

Emily went upstairs to the bathroom, took off all

her clothes, and wrapped herself in a striped towel. Then she bent over the sink and wet her hair, so that it lay dark and straight against her forehead. When she had finished, the person who gazed back at her from the mirror was not Emily at all, but an unknown girl from a faraway land.

Down the stairs she went, and out along the garden path, walking slowly in her bare feet. Mr Prendergast was waiting for her by the candlestick and the bowl. "Mr Prendergast," said Emily, "this is the best game we have ever played."

"Game?" said Mr Prendergast. "It is not a game."

"But Mr Prendergast," said Emily, "what do we do?"

"You must dance for me," said Mr Prendergast, and he began to sway gently from side to side once more. As Emily gazed at him she thought she heard the sound of the little bells, and the clash of the little cymbals. She closed her eyes, the music became louder, and slowly she began to dance. As she danced she felt that she really was a little Egyptian girl, with the sun burning down on her head, and with soft golden sand instead of grass between her toes. Then faster and faster she went, until the towel slipped, her foot caught in the folds; and down she went, knocking the candlestick against the bowl.

The bowl broke neatly into two halves, and the water spread out round Mr Prendergast. "Phhttt!" he said, and ran off a little way. The spell was broken, and he was no longer a god. He was just a cat who had got his feet wet, and he stood shaking first one paw and then another. Then he glanced idly at the broken bowl, as though it didn't concern him, and began to stroll away. As he went, he still shook a back leg from time to time, like a person who has got a sticky piece of paper stuck to their shoe.

Emily ran after him. She was very angry with him. As soon as a thing was finished he forgot all about it, and turned his thoughts to something else. Now he was on his way to the elderberry bush, which was his favourite place for sleeping. He left the ruined temple behind him, as though it had never been, and Emily was no longer an Egyptian girl, dancing in the sun — she was just an ordinary child in a garden, holding a muddy towel. "I shan't change myself for *you* any more!" she shouted into the bush. But Mr

Prendergast only looked at her sleepily, from between the branches. "I didn't ask you to," he said.

Emily picked up the broken bowl and the candlestick, and went back to the house. Her mother was very cross with her — but it was impossible to explain about the temple. When she was dressed and the bowl mended she took her mother down to the bottom of the garden. "See!" she said, setting the candlestick down in the grass, "it was a little temple for Mr Prendergast."

But it is no use trying to call back an enchanted time. The sun had moved over the sky, and the candlestick no longer shone in the sun. The grass where it stood was wet and flat, the spiders' webs and dandelion clocks were scattered, and Mr Prendergast himself lay sleeping in the bush, like any other tabby cat.

Emily didn't see him for the rest of the day, but when night time came, he leapt through the open window, and stood at the bottom of her bed, gazing

at her. "The candlestick is still in the garden," he said. "Come and dance for me again."

But Emily just shook her head. "No," she said, "I'm not an Egyptian girl. I'm just me — Emily."

For a moment she thought that he was offended, and that he wouldn't love her if she didn't change for him. But he merely gave a little flick of his tail. "Yes, you are," he said, "but I still rather like you."

And with that, he jumped back on to the window sill, and vanished.

6

The Birthday

Early one morning, Emily woke up to find Mr Prendergast sitting in her bed and staring at her. "Today is my birthday," he said, "I thought it best to inform you as soon as possible, so that we could begin the celebrations."

Emily sat up at once. "Why didn't you tell me before that today was your birthday?" she said.

"I didn't know myself until I woke up," said Mr Prendergast. He began to knead the bedclothes with his two front paws, and his purr was high and loud, like the sound of water boiling briskly in a kettle. "You know how it is," he said. "One wakes up with that certain feeling. Aha! you cry, today's the day! Today's my birthday!"

"But I always know when my birthday will be," said Emily.

"How exceedingly boring for you," said Mr Prendergast.

"It isn't boring at all!" said Emily, and she told him all about her last birthday; about the birthday cards, the presents, and the birthday cake with its candles.

Mr Prendergast listened politely. "My birthday will be much better," he said. "I don't know *what* will happen, but whatever it is, it will be something wonderful." He leapt up on to the sill and out through the window, eager to begin his birthday celebrations. Emily ran down the stairs to join him, and found him waiting for her on the doorstep. "What do you think might happen?" she asked.

"Oh, friends and acquaintances will arrive and sing me a special birthday song," he said carelessly. "That seems to me to be the kind of thing that should happen at the start of one's birthday."

He trotted off over the garden, and Emily followed him. The dew lay heavy on the grass, and by the time they reached the fence the legs of Emily's pyjamas were soaked. Mr Prendergast's fur was as sleek as a seal's, but he seemed not to care at all, and sat gazing out to where, some little way along the lane, a large brown rabbit sat twitching its nose.

Mr Prendergast pricked his ears, as though he was listening intently, but Emily could hear nothing at all. "Is he a friend or acquaintance?" she asked. "Is he singing you a special birthday song?"

"I've never seen him before in my life," said Mr Prendergast, with a look of disgust. "And he is singing 'Grass is green and burrows are deep' — which is about him, and not about me." He said "Phhttt!" several times, and batted the blades of grass with his paw, which made both himself and Emily wetter than ever.

Emily felt sorry for him. He had expected such a wonderful start to his birthday, but all that had happened was that a rabbit had sung him a rather dull song, and he had got very wet.

"I'll sing you a birthday song!" said Emily, and she sang, "Happy birthday to you, happy birthday to you, happy birthday, dear Mr Prendergast, happy birthday to you!"

"That wasn't very special," said Mr Prendergast, when the song ended. "Why didn't you sing 'Hurrah! Here is Mr Prendergast, walking about the world! Here is Prendergast, thinking his thoughts! Mr Prendergast's thoughts are like butterflies. They spread their wings and are beautiful!'" His purr grew louder and higher as he sang (for he could sing and purr at the same time) and then he stopped and

64

looked at her sternly. "Why haven't you invented a song like that?" he said.

Emily didn't answer; it is impossible to explain why you haven't invented a certain song. You just haven't and that is all there is to it. The legs of her pyjamas began to feel cold and clammy, and she left Mr Prendergast sitting by the fence and went back to the house.

She felt rather annoyed with him, but later that morning, she looked out of the kitchen window, and saw him sitting sadly in the middle of the path. He was hanging his head, and he was no longer the proud and joyous cat who had trotted out into the dewy morning, expecting something wonderful to happen.

Emily began to look in the kitchen drawers for something that she might take to him as a birthday present, for what can be nicer than to see someone coming down the garden path towards you, smiling, and carrying something neatly wrapped and tied with a ribbon bow.

She looked for a long time, and at last found a little ball. It was as clear as glass, but with a lovely swirl of colours in the middle. It was one of Emily's most favourite things, for when you threw it to the ground, it bounced much higher than you would expect a small ball to bounce. It was almost magical in the way that it soared up, and it surprised Emily every time it did it.

She wrapped it quickly, tied it with a ribbon and ran down the path to where Mr Prendergast sat gazing mournfully at a weed which grew between the paving stones. "For you," she said, laying the little parcel before him. "Happy birthday."

Mr Prendergast scrabbled the paper from his present with his paw, and Emily took the little ball and bounced it as hard as she could. Up it went, like a small, round, whirling rainbow. Mr Prendergast gazed at it, and Emily saw his eyes grow wide with amazement. Then down the little ball came, and vanished into the long grass. Emily went to look for it, but it was nowhere to be found. Mr Prendergast sat on the path and watched her. "Thank you," he said, when at last she returned to him. "Thank you for that brief moment of magic."

"Very brief," he added as he marched off and sat down in a clump of delphiniums.

Emily knelt and peered through the flower stalks. She could see little of him, other than the tip of his twitching tail, but she could hear his voice quite clearly. "One would think," he said, "that on one's birthday there would be something a little more *lasting*."

"Oh, *really*," said Emily, and she got up and marched back to the kitchen.

She saw little of him for the rest of the day, but she thought about him a great deal. When teatime came, and the garden began to grow dark, she stopped feeling annoyed with him, and decided that at least he must have a birthday cake, for he hadn't had a happy day at all — no friends had come to sing him a special song, and his birthday present had been lost.

"Oh, Emily," said Emily's mother, "what a fuss you make of that cat." But she found a small cake, and a pink candle left over from Emily's last birthday. When the candle was lit, Emily carried the cake to the bottom of the garden, and set it down before Mr Prendergast. As he bent to look at it, she saw the little flame of the candle reflected in his eyes.

It was a magical moment; but like all magical moments, it quickly passed, for it was time for Emily's own tea, and her mother was calling to her from the kitchen door.

When at last she hurried back down the garden she found that Mr Prendergast's friends and acquaintances had at last been to share his birthday, for the cake had been taken from its fluted paper case, and pieces of it were scattered about the grass. Some pieces had quite large bites taken out of them, while others had been merely nibbled at with small sharp teeth. Someone had even eaten half of the pink candle.

Emily wondered who the friends had been and what they had said and done. As she sat holding the chewed candle, Mr Prendergast came strolling to her side. He seemed happy and peaceful, and they sat together in silence for a time, and gazed up at the stars.

"It's just that a birthday is such an extraordinary thing," said Mr Prendergast at last, as though trying to explain his bad behaviour. "There's the world, whirling through space for years and years without you — and then, quite suddenly *there you are*. One somehow expects something special to happen when the day comes round again."

Emily knew exactly what he meant; it was an amazing and mysterious thing to have happened, and she wanted him to explain it to her; but when she turned to him, she found that he had wandered off a little way, and was patting something in the grass with his paw. It was the birthday ball, and watching him Emily knew that already he had

69

forgotten about the spinning world, and the time when they were not in it.

"Well, who ate the birthday cake candle?" she shouted after him — but he didn't answer that question either, and just ran off over the garden, chasing the ball, and thinking his butterfly thoughts.

7

An Adventurous Time Together

"We are going to spend a weekend at Auntie's caravan," said Emily's mother at breakfast. "We'll have a lovely time, just the four of us."

"Five," said Emily, "Mr Prendergast can come too." The last time she had gone on holiday she had left him sitting quietly on the roof of his little holiday house; but what stories he had told her on his return — what wild adventures he had had, each one wilder and more exciting than the one before. If she left him again, she thought, he might go off on an adventure and never come back.

"But Emily," said her mother, "you can't take a cat to the seaside."

"Yes, you *can*!" said Emily. "He's *got* to come with us!"

Emily's mother and father looked at Emily and then at one another. "Well," they said, "it's a nice, quiet place . . . It might be all right . . . "

"It will be wonderful!" said Emily, and she ran out into the garden to tell Mr Prendergast. Mr Prendergast was sitting by the fence, washing his face, with his eyes closed.

"You're coming on holiday with us," said Emily, "to Auntie's caravan."

For a moment Mr Prendergast continued to flick his paw over his nose. Then he opened his eyes and smiled. "Auntiescaravan," he said, all in one word. Emily wondered if he thought that that was the name of the place; but she didn't stop to try to explain the matter to him. She picked him up, and ran back to the house with him, to show her mother and father how pleased he was to be going on holiday with them. But when she dropped him to the floor, he didn't jump back up on his springy paws, but just lay there, all limp and smiling, saying "Auntiescaravan" in a silly manner.

"Well, really!" said Emily.

The next day she packed her bag, and got out Mr Prendergast's travelling basket. He had nothing at all to pack except his catnip mouse. He was very fond of his mouse, and sometimes lay on his back, and juggled with it, with all four paws. The mouse's whiskers and tail were gone, and he was nothing more than a piece of grey stuffed felt, but Mr Prendergast loved him.

So Emily carefully wrapped the mouse in a piece of tissue paper, and placed him in a corner of the basket.

"Oh, Emily," said Emily's mother.

"It's his *luggage*," said Emily, "he's got to have a proper holiday, just like us."

The next day everyone went to Auntie's caravan. It stood in a field of long grass. Beyond the edge of the field was a little lane which led to the sand dunes. On the other side of the dunes was the quiet little bay, with its golden sand and murmuring sea. Emily carried her bucket and spade in one hand, and Mr Prendergast over her other arm. "When we get to the beach, I will make you a wonderful sandcastle," said Emily. "Will you like that?"

"Yes," said Mr Prendergast — but when she set him down on the beach, he turned and went back to the dunes.

For a time Emily wandered about looking for him. Sometimes she saw the tip of his tail waving to and fro, over the top of a sand hill, and sometimes she came upon him suddenly, lying in a little warm hollow, and purring. But always, when she bent to pick him up, he slipped away from her and disappeared.

Emily went back to the beach, to where her

mother and father sat behind the red windbreak, and where Daniel lay on his rug, watching the seagulls fly past. "Mr Prendergast isn't having his holiday properly at all," she said, "he's just being silly."

"Perhaps he's having a good time in his own way," said Emily's mother.

"But I wanted us to have a good time together," said Emily crossly. She picked up her spade and began to make the sandcastle. More families had come to the beach, and the children ran shouting to the edge of the sea. From time to time, Emily looked at them, and wondered if she should go with them; but then she thought of how pleased Mr Prendergast would be with his castle and of how he would sit proudly in it, when it was finished. She made towers and walls and ramparts, and decorated them with pebbles and shells.

But Mr Prendergast stayed in the sand dunes. Sometimes, when Emily turned her head, she saw him looking at her between the blades of sea-grass. But he didn't come down to the beach, and by and by the tide began to come in. Emily's family collected their things, folded up the red windbreak, and began to make their way back over the dunes.

Mr Prendergast was waiting for them and he rubbed himself against Emily's ankles. Emily picked him up, and they stood and watched as the waves came up the beach and began to wash away the walls of the castle. "It was for *you*," said Emily — but Mr Prendergast didn't seem to care, or even hear her. Emily turned and ran to where her family plodded over the sand hills, with Daniel waving gaily over her father's shoulder. "I had a jolly nice day!" said Mr Prendergast, bumping against her knees as he went.

But Emily was so cross with him that she didn't speak to him for the rest of the day. She sat on the caravan steps and watched as he rolled about in the grass, tossing his catnip mouse in the air.

"He's enjoying his holiday," said Emily's father.

"But he's having it on his *own*," said Emily, "I wanted him to have it with *me*, but he went off and had adventures by himself."

That night she lay in her bunk, and waited for Mr Prendergast to come and tell her the story of his adventures. But when he came, he merely sat on her foot, and said "Auntiescaravan" as though it was a joke, and he was waiting for her to laugh.

Emily sat up and looked at him, and saw that he was smiling. He had spent a secret, happy day all by himself, and he was thinking about it. But I want us to be happy *together*, thought Emily.

"Tomorrow," she said, "I'll make you another sandcastle."

"Thank you," said Mr Prendergast.

But the next morning, when Emily and her family went down to the beach, Mr Prendergast just ran straight back into the sand dunes. Emily watched him go, then turned and began to make the new sandcastle. She made tower after tower, and didn't look back once to see if he was watching her. When she had finished, she marched to the dunes, found him sitting in a clump of sea pinks, grasped him firmly round the middle, and carried him down to the beach.

He scarcely seemed to see the castle and just picked his way delicately between the little towers and ran off up the beach. "Come back!" shouted Emily; but he paid no attention to her, and went weaving his way through the groups of children, and picnic lunches set out on the sand.

Emily followed him, seeing from the corner of her eye the picnickers brushing Mr Prendergast's footprints from the lunch cloths and blowing the scattered sand from their sandwiches. Then she lost sight of him, and could only follow his footprints, which lay like a little row of daisy shapes pressed into the sand.

She found him at last, sitting by a pool by some rocks. He was purring contentedly and dabbling his paw in the clear water in which there swam some small, pale, sea-creatures.

Emily bent and picked him up: and it was only

when she turned and looked back up the beach that she realised how far from her family she had come. The red windbreak was just a little blob of colour in the distance.

Emily began to run. But the beach seemed very big, and no matter how hard she ran, the windbreak didn't seem to come any closer. Mr Prendergast lay as limp as an old fur scarf that you might find tucked away in a dusty box of odds and ends, in a junk shop. His front legs hung over his arm, his long body and back legs hung down in front of her, and he flopped to and fro as she ran. "Isn't this fun!" he said.

"No!" said Emily. "It isn't fun at all!" Then she ran by the groups of children, and the picnickers, and saw them looking at her, and heard the sound of their laughter. She felt very foolish, to be running along a sunny beach, clutching the great floppy body of a cat — and to make matters worse, he had slipped down in her arms until his tail almost touched her ankles. She hoisted him up, and grasped him more tightly than ever. "If I let you go, you'll just run off again, won't you?" she said.

"Yes," said Mr Prendergast, "I'm afraid that is what I would most likely do."

So after this truthful reply there was nothing that Emily could do but hold on to him as best she could, and run until she reached the red windbreak, and her family. They waved to her, but she just turned, and walked up the beach.

"Where are you going?" called her mother.

"To the sand dunes," said Emily.

On the top of a little hill, Emily and Mr Prendergast sat down, side by side. "The holiday is almost gone," said Emily. "And we haven't done *anything* together. Not one thing."

"But I am a *cat*," said Mr Prendergast, "and you are a *child*."

"Isn't there anything that is the same for both of us?" asked Emily.

"Of course," said Mr Prendergast, "there's sleeping, and dancing in the sun, and love, and playing with one's catnip mouse."

"I don't play with a catnip mouse," said Emily.

"Oh, you should," said Mr Prendergast, "it's great fun."

Emily flopped back on the sand. Below the hill, the children ran, shouting and laughing, and Emily remembered her burning cheeks and the awful feeling she had when everyone had looked at her. "There's not liking being laughed at," she said — but gazing up into his calm face and his golden eyes, she knew that he hadn't minded the laughter at all; for he did just what he wanted to, and didn't care what anyone thought. He lived his own life, and found things for himself that made him happy, like the little pool amongst the rocks. And now that she had brought him back to the dunes, he was content with that too, and sat nibbling a blade of grass, and making his little jokes. "Auntiescaravan,"

he said, as she reached up and tickled him. He was just himself, Mr Prendergast, and she loved him.

For a moment longer she lay, stroking his warm tummy, and then she stood, and began to make her way back to the beach, to stick some more stones and shells on the walls of her castle. "Have a nice time," she said as she went.

"You too," said Mr Prendergast, as he strolled off over the dunes.

8

The Witch in the Wood

Emily was waiting for the arrival of her Aunt Harriet. It was a bright, windy day in autumn, and Emily had been in a great deal of trouble, one way or another. She was sitting sadly by the kitchen door when Mr Prendergast walked by. He looked unconcerned, and there was a little smile on his face.

Emily watched him go. "Mr Prendergast is never in trouble!" she thought, and got up, and went along the garden path, kicking up the dead leaves. As she walked along, Mr Prendergast came by again, sleek and shining, and still smiling. "We will take a little walk after tea," he said, "and I will tell you the story of my life."

"Mr Prendergast," said Emily, "Why won't you speak to everyone? If you spoke to everyone, perhaps I shouldn't get into so much trouble."

"It wouldn't do," said Mr Prendergast, "I have thought about it, and I am forced to say that it just wouldn't do."

"Well, it isn't fair!" said Emily. "It just isn't fair!"

Mr Prendergast was very offended indeed. "I see," he said. "Cats do not choose to speak to anyone, you know. In fact, there are few persons in this world with whom a cat will choose to speak. I shall not speak to *you* again."

He ran off down the garden. Emily ran after him, and found him sitting in the spot where they had sat on that long-ago summer's day when he had worn his napkin-shawl and told her about the fish. With a sigh, she sat down beside him. "It's just that I get into so *much* trouble," she said. "If you would just explain!" But Mr Prendergast merely looked at her, then turned his head away.

"Please!" said Emily. "*I* speak to everyone, and it's really quite easy."

"*You* are a child," said Mr Prendergast, "*I* am a cat"; and with that he rose, slipped through the gap in the fence and trotted off down the lane.

Emily didn't see him again for the rest of the morning. In the afternoon, Aunt Harriet arrived, and everyone went for a walk before tea. They followed the little footpath that led over the field. Emily's mother and Aunt Harriet talked together as they walked, and after a while Emily left them, and ran ahead to the wood.

The trees grew thick at the edge of the wood, but once past the first trees, there lay a little grassy glade, so still and quiet that small animals and birds used it as a meeting place and a playground. And there, in the middle of the sunny glade, sat Mr Prendergast, with brown rabbits bobbing all about him, and with a blackbird singing on the branch above his head.

"Oh!" cried Emily. She felt that she had discovered a secret and enchanted place; but as soon as she stepped forward from the trees, everyone stopped what they were doing, and sat very still. For a moment, it was as if they were animals in a painting; then the rabbits turned and scurried to their burrows, the blackbird flew from the tree with a loud flap of his wings, and Mr Prendergast disappeared into the thick trees and bushes.

Emily ran after him. Just before she ran in amongst the dark trees, she turned and saw her mother, Aunt Harriet and Daniel come into the little glade, then on she ran, calling Mr Prendergast's name as she went. She meant to go only a little way, for she felt sure that she would soon come across Mr Prendergast, and that they would make up their quarrel. But, without knowing what she did, she strayed from the path, and when she tried to find it again, it was nowhere to be seen. Above her head, the branches of the trees grew so close together that she could scarcely see the sky.

"Mr Prendergast!" shouted Emily, as loudly as she could, "I'm lost!"

But there was no Mr Prendergast to appear by her side, saying in his calm, kind way, "*I am never lost.*" Then, as Emily sat, listening for the sound of his voice, she heard the faint rustling of twigs, and turning her head, she saw the witch in the bush.

She was a small, bent, thin little witch, huddled into a tattered black cloak, and her long fingers clutched at the branches of the bush as she tried to free herself.

With a scream, Emily ran, hearing behind her what she felt sure was the thump-thump of a pair of long black cracked leather boots. She stumbled over roots of trees as she went, ducked under the low

branches of trees; but the spiky branches of bushes seemed to grasp at her, and the wind in the leaves seemed to be saying "Let us catch her — catch her — catch her." It was as if the whole wood was in league with the witch, and at any moment Emily would feel a hand come down on her shoulder, like a little bundle of thin bones. Emily's stomach felt icy, and she found it hard to breathe; but there is only one thing to be done when you are so afraid, and that is to stop running and stand your ground.

Emily stopped, and slowly turned; and as if by magic, the path now lay before her. It was completely empty, and there, at the very end, like something glimpsed through a long dark tunnel, was the bright little glade where the rabbits hopped and the blackbird sang. Some distance down the lane, Mr Prendergast stepped from behind a bush, and at the sight of him the last trace of Emily's fear completely vanished. What was the witch but a tattered black rag and some yellow bones, that had no more power to hold her than a few dried flower stalks. Let this collection of rags and bones jump from the trees and try to frighten me, she thought as she ran to her cat. Me and Mr Prendergast will just say, "Go away!"

But when at last she reached his side, she stopped and stared, for he looked so odd, and not like himself at all. "Mr Prendergast — it's *me*," she said, but he only stared back at her, and the expression on his tiger-face was quite blank; it wasn't even the icy stare he gave her when he was offended. He was just a cat without any magic whatsoever. Emily picked him up and began to make her way down the path. In case the witch was hiding behind a tree or bush, she began to sing as loudly as she could. "Rag bone, rag bone!" she shouted, to show that she wasn't afraid. Still chanting, and clutching Mr Prendergast, she marched into the sunny glade where her mother and Aunt Harriet sat, with Daniel on his blue rug. When they saw Emily they smiled. "Isn't Emily *funny*?" said Aunt Harriet to Daniel, tickling his tummy — and there was no way in which Emily could explain why she shouted 'Rag bone!'', how she had run in terror from a witch, and how the magic of her dearest friend had suddenly and completely vanished.

*

That night Emily was awakened by the tapping of Mr Prendergast's paw on the tip of her nose. "It was an umbrella," he said, when Emily sat up and looked at him. His eyes were lit by the glow of the night-light, and they looked bigger and more golden than ever. "The witch in the wood," he said, "it was an old umbrella. I thought you might like to know."

He settled down on her knee and began to purr loudly. He was the old magical Mr Prendergast and

it was lovely to have him back; but Emily couldn't help thinking about how different he had seemed when she had run with him down the dark tunnel of trees.

"It is simply that, just as some people have moments of magic, I have moments of being quite ordinary," he said, when she asked about this. "It makes quite a pleasant change."

"Well, *really!*" said Emily, tumbling him off her knee — but he merely strolled to the end of the bed, and smiled at her in his gentle way. "But aren't you proud to think how brave you were, and all by yourself?" he said.

"I suppose so," said Emily, for suddenly she knew that if she was ever afraid again, she had only to think of how she had run until she had reached the sunny glade, and that sometimes what you are afraid of is nothing more than old umbrella, caught in a bush and flapping in the wind.

It is wonderful to make these discoveries, and Emily smiled at Mr Prendergast, thinking how wise he was, how clever, and how it didn't matter at all that he spoke only to her; he helped her understand such mysterious and exciting things. Eager for the next discovery, she scrambled down to the end of the bed.

But when she got there, she found that already he had decided to have another ordinary moment, and was gazing blankly into space.

9

Mr Prendergast's Education

Mr Prendergast was very clever, but he had never been to school.

"I have never been educated," he said. "It is my everlasting regret. I would have been a fine scholar!"

"What would you learn if you could?" asked Emily.

"Well," said Mr Prendergast, gazing round the garden, "there are so many things to study! I would study the reason for the days being sometimes cold, and sometimes hot. I would study flowers and insects, French, dancing, music, hill-climbing, the sea . . ."

"What a lot of things!" said Emily. But Mr Prendergast said crossly, "I haven't finished yet! I would study the question of why some things are fun, and some are not. After that, I would study elephants, and poetry, ants, and jam-making . . ."

The list went on and on. Emily fell asleep, and only awoke when her mother called her in for tea. Mr Prendergast was still reciting the list of things which he would like to study. "Fish!" he said, "and filing! Pig-rearing! Bell-ringing! Crocheting! . . ."

"Mr Prendergast!" said Emily — for he seemed to be beside himself. "Wellington boots!" he shouted. "Mud! Mystery! Movement!"

Emily went into the house, for she was very hungry. When she came out again, Mr Prendergast was sitting in a tree. Emily looked up at him. "Have you finished?" she said.

"No," said Mr Prendergast. "There's mat-making, clock-mending, and the question of why you are you, and not a cat, and why I am me and not you."

"*Why* am I me and not you?" asked Emily.

"Ah!" said Mr Prendergast. "There is no answer to that question!"

Emily could make no sense of him.

Emily's next door neighbour came to the garden

fence. "Your cat seems restless to me," she said. "He's seemed restless all day. Cats are apt to wander when they are restless, you know. You should butter his paws." She went into her kitchen, and came back with a little pat of butter, which she gave to Emily.

"I've never heard of such a thing!" said Emily.

Mr Prendergast said "Phhttt!" and came down from the tree, and ran off down the garden. It took Emily a long time to catch him, as he went faster and faster, and became more excited as he went. "Why is the moon round?" he said, as he raced up and down the path. "Why is there a moon at all? Why stars? Why questions? . . ."

But at last Emily flung herself upon him, and there, behind a dark green bush, she buttered his paws, saying, "There! Poor dear Mr Prendergast — now you'll feel better!"

They sat side by side, and Mr Prendergast licked his toes. After a while he said that he did indeed feel better, and that it had been very good butter. Then he jumped up on to the window sill, and dropped through the open window, into the living room.

Emily climbed after him, and found him sitting in front of the bookshelves.

"I could get my education now," said Mr Prendergast, "I've nothing at all to do after tea."

His voice was soft, and his eyes were dreamy, and he rubbed his head against her hand. "Take down the books, and prop them up as I tell you," he said.

"Oh, Mr Prendergast," said Emily, "*should* we. . . ?"

"Of course," said Mr Prendergast. "It will be purrrfectly all right. And I might find speaking to everyone quite easy, you know, once I've received my education."

"That would be wonderful!" said Emily.

Mr Prendergast sat on the sofa and watched as Emily took the books from the shelves, and propped them open round the room. It took a long time, but at last the shelves were empty.

"And now," said Mr Prendergast, jumping down from the sofa, "I shall merely walk past each book — starting at A and finishing with Z! But," he added, "before I begin, I might just mention that I feel a little restless — as though I might begin to wander, you know . . ."

So Emily went to the kitchen and brought back some butter, and buttered his paws. When Mr Prendergast had licked up all the butter, he began his education. He started with Architecture, and then went on to Bees.

Emily sat very still and quiet. She tried not to disturb him, but from time to time she whispered, "Are you learning a lot, Mr Prendergast?"

"I am learning a great deal, thank you," said Mr Prendergast, weaving round the table legs on his buttery paws. He had just started on Law, when the door opened and Emily's mother came into the room. "Oh — Emily!" she said.

That night, Emily lay in bed and gazed tearfully at Mr Prendergast. "I don't always know a thing is naughty, until I've done it," she said. "Then someone comes, and says 'Oh, *Emily* . . .'"

"When you've grown up a little things will be easier," said Mr Prendergast in his comforting voice. "Then you will be able to tell for yourself."

Emily sat and hugged him. Things didn't seem so bad with Mr Prendergast to keep her company. "Are you pleased that you got your education?" she asked.

"I am," said Mr Prendergast. He folded his paws, and gazed at her fondly. "An education is a wonderful thing," he said, "it helps you to think."

"Are you thinking *now*?" asked Emily, hoping

98

that he was thinking about the problem of whether or not he should speak to everyone.

"I am," said Mr Prendergast, "I am thinking deeply."

"What are you thinking about?" asked Emily.

"Butter," said Mr Prendergast.

10

The Smile

Emily wasn't at all sure if she liked her little brother until the day he smiled at her. Before, whenever she had bent over his cot or pram, he had merely gazed up as though she wasn't there at all, or he looked past her shoulder, as though there was something far more interesting behind her.

But one sunny day, Emily's mother took him out to the garden and laid him on his blue rug, in the shade of the tree. As Emily sat beside him, he looked up, suddenly, and smiled at her. It was a wonderful smile, like the smile of someone who has just made a delightful discovery. Emily was so pleased that she laughed aloud. Before, Daniel had just been a bundle in a blanket, but now he was a person.

Emily jumped up, and ran down to the bottom of

the garden to tell Mr Prendergast. He was sitting by a bush, watching the butterflies settle on the leaves. "Daniel *smiled* at me!" Emily told him proudly. She sat down beside him, and lifted him into her lap. To her surprise he didn't curl up, but went all stiff, and stepped back over her knees. "Did you tell him a joke?" he said.

"Of course not," said Emily.

"Did you perhaps sing him an amusing song?" said Mr Prendergast.

"No," said Emily.

"Then he must have been laughing at *you*," said Mr Prendergast coldly.

"He wasn't laughing at me," said Emily. "He was pleased to see me."

"Indeed!" said Mr Prendergast. "Did he say so? Did he say 'How very charmed to make your acquaintance'?"

Then he marched off into a clump of long grass, and sat with just the tips of his ears showing.

Emily knelt and parted the thick green blades, and looked at her cat. "Don't be silly," she said. "He can't talk yet. He just smiled."

"I can smile too," said Mr Prendergast, "but I don't care to at the moment."

"Why?" asked Emily. But Mr Prendergast didn't reply, and trotted off over the garden with his tail held stiff and erect.

Emily went back to where Daniel lay on his rug. He was holding his hands up before his face and was looking at them as though they didn't really belong to him at all, but were just something very interesting that happened to be there. Imagine not knowing that your hands belong to you! thought Emily, and she jumped up again to find Mr Prendergast, for surely this would make him smile.

But Mr Prendergast merely yawned. "Poor pink thing," he said, and curled himself into a ball, as if he was going to sleep — but he was only pretending, Emily knew, for when she turned to look back at him she saw that his eyes were upon her and that he was watching her narrowly as she sat down on Daniel's blanket.

Daniel began to blow spit-bubbles. He did this quite suddenly, as though the idea had just occurred to him, and he got very excited and waved his arms about. Emily laughed. The sound roused Mr Prendergast, and he came over the grass and across the corner of the blue blanket. "Fish," he said coldly, as he passed.

"He isn't a fish," said Emily.

Mr Prendergast came back, and stared at Daniel.

"He *thinks* he's a fish," he said, looking at the bubbles and the waving arms.

"No, he doesn't," said Emily. "He doesn't know what he is yet. He's only just beginning to find out."

"Then let us hope that he comes to the right conclusion," said Mr Prendergast. "It wouldn't be very nice for you to find that you had a fish for a brother." He smiled at her before going up the garden, but it wasn't a very nice smile.

In the afternoon, Emily's mother said that Emily could give Daniel his bottle. Emily was very pleased, and she sat proudly on the blue rug, with Daniel in the crook of her arm. He gazed steadily at her, as he sucked his bottle — but there was another pair of eyes upon her; for when Emily looked up, she saw Mr Prendergast glaring at her from behind the kitchen window. He had thrust his head through a busy-lizzie plant, and small red flowers were festooned around his ears. He looked rather silly, and Emily laughed.

Daniel finished his bottle, and she laid him carefully on the rug, and began to make her way to the house. But as she ran down the path, Mr Prendergast disappeared from the window. She found him, some time later, sitting under the kitchen dresser. He had found a ball of fluff, and was patting it to and fro, but he didn't seem to be very interested in the game.

"Come outside and play," said Emily.

"Thank you, no," said Mr Prendergast. "I prefer to stay here. By myself. In the dark. For ever and ever."

"But you can't possibly stay under the dresser for ever!" said Emily. Mr Prendergast ignored her. "Ahhh . . ." he said, sighing deeply, "for some it's all sunshine and smiles — but for others, what is life but a ball of fluff?" He gazed at his fluff-ball, as if it was the one poor pleasure left in his life. Then he sighed again, so loud and strongly that he blew the fluff-ball from under the dresser, and it bowled gaily over the kitchen floor.

Emily bit her lip, to keep herself from laughing — for she knew now that, sorry for himself though he was, Mr Prendergast's feelings were very real: and when someone feels something so strongly, you must do your best to help and understand them, even if they express their feelings in what seems to you to be a rather silly way.

She reached out her hand, grasped him firmly, and pulled him from under the dresser. He came out squatting on his haunches, and at first he wouldn't look at her or speak. But after she had stroked his head for a time, he said, in a little careless voice, "Do you still love me, now that you've got a baby brother?"

"Of course I love you," said Emily. "It's just that I love Daniel now as well. I didn't think I did until he smiled at me. It was a lovely surprise!"

"If he smiles at me, will I love him too?" said Mr Prendergast. "Will I have a lovely surprise?"

"I'm sure you will," said Emily.

She picked him up, and carried him to where Daniel lay on his rug.

Daniel had been asleep, but he opened his eyes, looked up at Emily and Mr Prendergast, and gave his wonderful crooked smile. Mr Prendergast began to

purr loudly. Then he scrambled up on to Emily's shoulder. "Does he know that I'm a cat?" he murmured in her ear. "Does he know that *I* am *Mr Prendergast?*"

"Not yet," said Emily, "but when he's older we shall tell him. When he's old enough, we shall tell him all about you!"

11

Mr Prendergast's House

Mr Prendergast's house was very beautiful, but he did not build it himself. It came about in this way. It was two days before Christmas and the snow was falling fast. Emily was excited and happy. The big tree was in its tub in the corner, and the decorations lay in their box on the dresser, waiting to be hung. On the sofa were blue, green, and golden boxes, waiting to be filled with presents for the friends and relations who would visit on Christmas day.

Mr Prendergast sat on the rug before the fire, and Emily sat beside him. "Mr Prendergast," she said, "what would you like most of all for Christmas?"

"I should like a house," said Mr Prendergast. "A house of my own."

"A house!" said Emily, looking at him in surprise.

"It will be quite easy," said Mr Prendergast. "I

shall tell you how I should like my house to be built, and you shall build it for me."

"A *house*!" said Emily again.

Mr Prendergast ignored her remark. "First," he said, "you will take the big red box from the sofa — that will be my living room. Then you will take the blue and silver box for my bedroom. At the top of my house, I will have the green box with the stars. It will be my thinking room."

So Emily brought the tube of glue from the kitchen. She brought the boxes from the sofa, and the coloured glass balls from the dresser. Then, while Mr Prendergast sat on the rug and watched, she glued the boxes together.

"It is satisfactory," said Mr Prendergast, when the last box had been put in place, "it is quite satisfactory. Now we will decorate it."

Holding her breath, Emily laid the strips of tinsel over the roof, and hung the coloured balls from their strings so that they spun slowly before each of the rooms. "Your house is finished!" she said.

"But it must have a name," said Mr Prendergast.

So Emily went into the kitchen and cut words and

letters from the boxes and packets in the cupboards. She took the letters and words back to the living room, and laid them on the rug. Mr Prendergast sniffed at them. "Sandwich?" he said. "Margarine? Kelloggs? Those are not names for a house."

"Couldn't we just write 'Mr Prendergast's House' on a piece of paper?" asked Emily. Mr Prendergast said nothing to this. He was silent for a long time, and then he spoke. "I shall call my house 'San-Marga-Kello'," he said.

It was a beautiful name, thought Emily, as she snipped the words into pieces, and then stuck them back together again, to make the sign.

When the sign had been hung, Mr Prendergast jumped up into his thinking room, and closed his eyes. He sat there for a long time, purring loudly. Then his purr grew softer and softer, and his head sank lower and lower.

"Mr Prendergast!" said Emily.

Mr Prendergast opened his eyes, and looked at her. "I wasn't *sleeping*!" he said. "I was thinking and what I was thinking was this — The Distant Vista."

"*What?*" said Emily.

"Haven't you ever heard of it?" said Mr Prendergast. "It is said like this . . ." He sat upright in his green, starry room, so that his head touched the roof, and strips of tinsel fell on each side of his face. "From the windows could be seen the distant vista of rolling hills."

"But Mr Prendergast!" said Emily. "We can't make hills!"

"It doesn't have to be hills," said Mr Prendergast, "it might be the sea — or even a lake."

"But we can't make those either!" said Emily.

Mr Prendergast jumped from his house, and went to sit under the table. "Please come back to your lovely house," said Emily. But Mr Prendergast just shook his head. "Without a distant vista it is useless," he said. "That is the whole point of the thing. One sits in one's house, and contemplates the distant vista."

So Emily took the poker and tongs, and put them under the rug. She made a small mountain, and a bigger mountain behind it. Then she folded the rest of the rug, so that it looked like gently rolling hills. Mr Prendergast came back to his house, and Emily lay down beside it; together, in the firelight, they gazed at the mysterious mountains. "Please tell me a story," said Emily.

"Very well," said Mr Prendergast, and he began, "once upon a time, there was a princess called Emily, who lived in the far away mountains . . ."

But before he could go any further, the door of the living room was opened, and the light was switched

on. Mr Prendergast leapt from his house and vanished.

"Oh, Emily — just look at this mess!" cried Emily's mother.

Emily began to cry. In the glare of the light, the beautiful "San-Marga-Kello" was just a few boxes, sticky with glue, and the mysterious mountains were only the rug, with the poker and tongs beneath it.

That night as Emily lay in bed, Mr Prendergast crept softly to her pillow. He was carrying a glass ball by its piece of string. On the glass ball was stuck the word "San".

"Oh, Mr Prendergast!" said Emily, "your beautiful house, and your Distant Vista . . ."

Mr Prendergast placed the ball by her cheek. "It doesn't matter," he said, in his kindliest tone, "it was the kind of house one has only for a little while — and one can always see a distant vista, if one cares to look."

12

Friends

Emily was very shy, and she had always found it hard to make friends, until the day that Sara and Laura came to stay with their grandmother next door. Emily saw them arrive and go running up the path, and into the house; she saw them looking at her from an upstairs window, as she sat with Mr Prendergast on the lawn — a moment later, they stepped through the gap in the hedge which grew between the two gardens, and came towards her, smiling.

To Emily's surprise, Mr Prendergast didn't behave at all in the way that he usually behaved when strangers appeared. He didn't say "Phhttt!" He didn't run off, and glare at them from a bush. Instead, he went forward to meet them, walking with a high, delicate and dignified step, as though he were a host at a party, and they were his special guests.

Emily sat and watched as the little group came together, paused for a moment, as if in greeting, and then went their separate ways — Sara and Laura to where Emily sat in the shade of the tree, and Mr Prendergast to a clump of cool ferns. It was so nice to watch this little scene that Emily almost forgot to be shy.

To feel shy is to be very uncomfortable, to have a fluttering tummy and burning cheeks. But once someone has smiled at you, has told you their name, and made a remark about the beauty of your cat, the worst is over. To her delight, Emily found that she had made two friends, and that she had done it quite easily.

She felt extremely happy. For days the weather had been very hot, and she and Mr Prendergast had trailed listlessly about the garden. The heat made Mr Prendergast drowsy, and he hadn't told her any amusing stories, or suggested anything interesting that they might do together. He liked to find shady places to lie in, but Emily found this rather boring.

She had her paddling pool, and her swing which hung from a branch of the tree. "But cats," said Mr Prendergast, "neither swing nor paddle."

Now Emily had two friends. They jumped in the paddling pool with her, and made the water rise in great shining arcs over the grass. Then they ran, laughing, up and down the path, with buckets of water, refilled the pool, and jumped in again. At the end of the day, everyone had tea beneath the tree. When it was time to go, Sara and Laura walked back through the garden. By the gap in the hedge, they turned and waved their hands. "See you in the morning!" they said.

Emily went to find Mr Prendergast, to tell him about her lovely day, but he was nowhere to be seen. Emily wondered about this, but it was only a fleeting thought, for already she was looking forward to the next morning.

For the rest of the week, Emily played with Sara and Laura; but she saw little of Mr Prendergast. Sometimes she saw him strolling along the garden fence. Sometimes she caught the gleam of his golden eye, as he watched her from beneath the fronds of fern. (Once she saw him dancing in the long grass, jumping up with his back arched high, and his legs held straight.) Sometimes, when the three friends sat together under the tree, he strolled between them, lazy and elegant and sleepy with the sun. As he went, he and Emily smiled at one another; but they were the kind of smiles that you give someone who lives at the other end of the street — someone you see and like, but about whom you do not know a great deal. And, just as it does of people at the end of the street, the thought crossed Emily's mind that soon she would seek Mr Prendergast out, and they would have a good long talk.

But one by one the days went by, until it was time for Sara and Laura to go home. Emily waved goodbye to them as they went back through the gap in the hedge, and then at last she went to look for Mr Prendergast; for she had a great deal to tell him.

Mr Prendergast was nowhere to be found. Emily searched everywhere for him, but he was in none of his favourite places. The sight of the empty places made her feel sad. While she had played with her friends, her cat had been left alone. She thought of how he had sat by himself beneath the ferns. She thought of his solitary dance, and these thoughts made her very unhappy.

When evening came, she sat by her open window, and wondered if, because of his loneliness, he had gone to make a new life for himself. The more she thought of this, the more sure she became that this was what had happened. Mr Prendergast had gone. "Goodbye!" she whispered, trying to send her thoughts to him, wherever he might be. "Be happy!"

But as she gazed tearfully out over the moonlit garden, there suddenly leapt from a clump of grasses the arched and stiff-legged body of a dancing cat. It was Mr Prendergast, Emily knew that at once, and she ran down the stairs and out across the garden.

As she ran she saw him leap again and again; but when at last she reached him he was sitting quite still, and with his two front paws set primly side by side.

"What *are* you doing?" she asked. When you are so filled with happiness, it is useless to try to express how you feel. It is best to say something quite ordinary.

But as Emily sat by Mr Prendergast's side, she began to see, coming over the garden, the dark and graceful shapes of cats. Some were making curious little noises, like the faint chirruping of birds; some jumped suddenly sideways, on all four legs; some leapt as Mr Prendergast had done. Up they went, one after another, then out from between the rustling blades of grass they came, with gentle outstretched paws.

"Jones ... The Dairymaid ... Scraggs-Mulligan," said Mr Prendergast, murmuring the names as the cats passed by.

"But who are they, and what are they doing?" asked Emily, jumping to her feet — for who can sit and talk of ordinary things, when they find that the garden they sit in is full of chirruping, dancing cats.

Mr Prendergast just yawned and stretched himself. "They are friends," he said, "meeting on a summer's night — as we have done."

Emily sat down beside him again, and they were silent for a time. "I didn't think we'd ever meet again," she said, at last. "I thought you'd *gone*. I thought, 'I left him alone, and now he's gone for ever'."

"Gone for ever?" said Mr Prendergast. "Merely because I didn't care to paddle or swing?" He gazed at her steadily, with his unwinking golden eyes. "A cat is a cat," he said, in his firm but kind voice, "and a child is a child. We each have our own friends, and times when we do things differently."

"We do things together too!" said Emily, afraid that he was, after all, trying to say goodbye to her, was becoming an ordinary cat, like the time in the wood, when she had found him sitting as any cat might sit, and thinking thoughts that she could never know.

He mustn't say goodbye! she told herself, he mustn't become ordinary, for he was the secret, magical part of her life. "Mr Prendergast!" she cried, kneeling and stretching out her arms to him. But he merely sat before her, upright and serene.

"Think of it as a dance," he said. "Sometimes the steps lead us together, and sometimes they lead us apart — but always we are *together in the dance*."

It was a lovely thought, and Emily closed her eyes for a moment, and pictured the two of them dancing round the lawn in the sunshine. Then she rose and brushed the grass seeds from her knees; for she knew now that she must let Mr Prendergast go to his friends, as he had let her go to Laura and Sara.

A little way across the garden she looked back, and saw him strolling in the moonlight to where the cats sat in a great circle, making the curious little sounds, the calls, cries and murmurs with which they spoke to one another about their secret lives. Then she turned and went into the house, thinking of all the friends that she herself might make in the future — but that no matter how many there might be, there would never be one as wonderful, as loving, or as special as Mr Prendergast.